WHEN DAD CUTS DOWN
THE
CHESTNUT TREE

Written by
PAM AYRES

Illustrated by
GRAHAM PERCY

DISCOVERY TOYS

When Dad cuts down the chestnut tree,

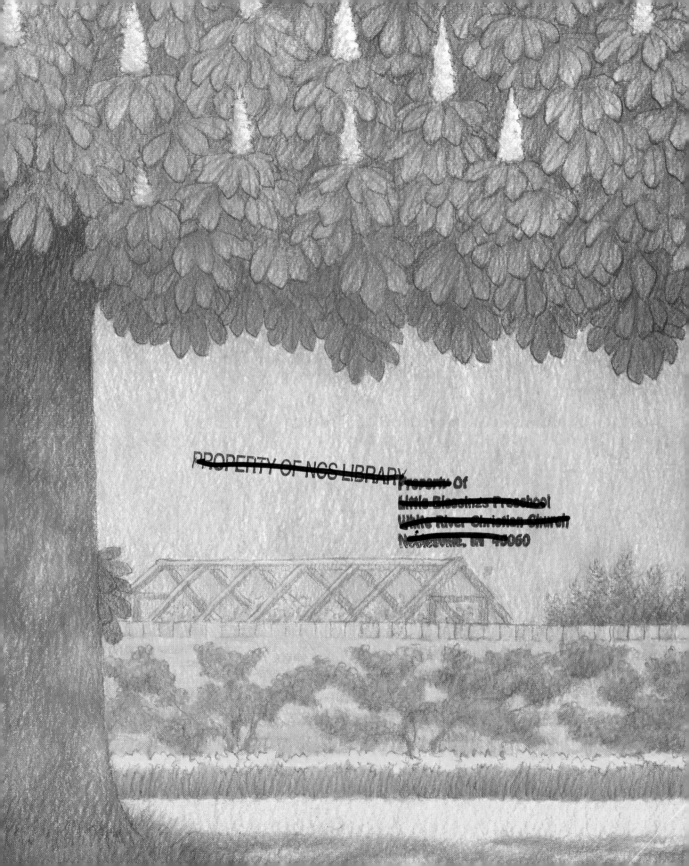

For James
P.A.

This edition is
published and distributed
exclusively by
DISCOVERY TOYS
Pleasant Hill, CA

Originally published by
Walker Books, Ltd.
London

Printed in Italy

1 2 3 4 5 6 7 8 9 0

ISBN 0-939979-14-4

He'll make such things for you and me…

A rocking horse to ride all day,

A fort where all my soldiers stay.

A wheelbarrow painted blue,

A faithful duck on wheels for you.

Stilts to make us very tall,

Colored blocks to build a wall.

When the tree is on the ground,
All my friends will come around.

On the trunk we'll jump and climb,
We will have a lovely time!

No more tearing jacket sleeves,

No more sweeping up of leaves.

And when I'm tucked into my bed,
Kisses kissed and goodnights said,

The tree won't scare me any more,
When the night wind makes it roar.

If there wasn't any tree
What difference would it make to me?

No tree house – that's the worst of all –
To hide in when we hear Mom call.

No cool places in the shade,
When we have run and jumped and played.

No leaves to kick and throw about
And roll each other in and shout.

No sticks to find on chilly days,
To make our winter fires blaze.

And there is another thing —
What will happen to our swing?

Where will owl and squirrel stay
If the tree is hauled away?

If the tree is really gone,
What can I hang my birdhouse on?

Suddenly we're not so sure
We want it cut down any more.

Trees are special, large or small,
So Dad – don't cut it down *at all!*